Charles R. Street, Henry C. Platt

## An Opinion upon the Powers and Duties

Of the trustees of the freeholders and commonalty of the town of

Huntington; especially with reference to lands under tide waters - the

oyster fisheries, and dock franchises, with a historical review of the early

Charles R. Street, Henry C. Platt

**An Opinion upon the Powers and Duties**
*Of the trustees of the freeholders and commonalty of the town of Huntington;
especially with reference to lands under tide waters - the oyster fisheries, and dock
franchises, with a historical review of the early*

ISBN/EAN: 9783337284435

Printed in Europe, USA, Canada, Australia, Japan

Cover: Foto ©Andreas Hilbeck / pixelio.de

More available books at **www.hansebooks.com**

# AN OPINION

UPON THE

# POWERS AND DUTIES

OF

# THE TRUSTEES

OF THE

# REEHOLDERS AND COMMONALTY

OF THE

# Town of Huntington;

ESPECIALLY WITH REFERENCE TO

inds under Tide Waters; the Oyster Fisheries, and Dock Franchises,

WITH A

# HISTORICAL REVIEW

OF THE

# EARLY SETTLEMENT OF THE TOWN.

By CHARLES R. STREET and HENRY C. PLATT,
*Counsellors at Law, Huntington, L. I.*

New York.
PRINTED BY JOHN DeVRIES, 112 & 114 WOOSTER STREET.
1879.

# 1871-2.

---

# Trustees of the Freeholders and Commonalty

OF THE

## TOWN OF HUNTINGTON.

---

**President.**

## STEPHEN K. GOULD.

**Trustees.**

CHARLES T. DURYEA,
ISAAC C. IRELAND,
ISAAC W. ROE,
PLATT KETCHAM,
BENJAMIN DOTY.
SELAH SMITH.

# PREFACE.

At an annual town meeting of the Town of Huntington, held on the 4th day of April, 1871, a Resolution was passed in open meeting authorizing and directing the Trustees of the Town to lease all the oyster grounds within the Town, and before making any such leases to consult and obtain the opinion of counsel as to what particular oyster grounds the Town has control over, and as to the best and safest manner of making such leases.

At a meeting of the Trustees, at which there was a full attendance, on the 8th day of May, 1871, the following resolution was passed by the Board:

*Resolved:* That the President of the Board employ counsel, on behalf of the Board, to investigate and give an opinion as to the powers and duties of the Trustees, respecting the rights of the Town to lands under tide waters, and to have the same printed.

Pursuant to such authority, the Board of Trustees employed the undersigned to give an opinion in writing upon the points stated in the above resolution.

In collecting materials for an opinion we found it necessary to examine the records, as to the ancient charters and grants, in the office of the Secretary of State, at Albany, and to carefully examine the records and papers in the Clerk's office of the Town of Huntington, and we cheerfully testify to the prompt and valuable aid rendered us by the Deputy Secretary of State, Diedrich Willers, Jr., and the obliging Clerk of the Town, Daniel L. Baylis. We are, also, under obligations to the Librarian of the New York City Library, for the convenient access furnished to its rare and very full collection of ancient text-books and Reports of English Cases bearing upon the subject.

We submit the following opinion as embodying our views upon the subjects embraced within the inquiry submitted to us.

CHARLES R. STREET,
HENRY C. PLATT.

*January* 1, 1872.

# OPINION.

The powers and duties of the Trustees of the Freeholders and Commonalty of the Town of Huntington, are measured by the express letter of written law and, also, by the uniform and well settled principles which control public officers invested with the quality of Trustees, as authoritively expounded by the Courts. As Trustees, they stand in the place of the people, the Freeholders and Commonalty of the Town, to act in trust in and about all such matters as they may lawfully act, in acquiring, managing and disposing of the public property.

In order to ascertain what their powers and duties are and the way and manner in which those powers should be exercised, we must necessarily extend our inquiries over a wide range. The written law no where fully describes or defines the powers and duties of the Trustees with certainty, for the reason that the subjects about which their duties are required, or upon which the exercise of their powers are properly invoked, may or may not exist according to circumstances. Though their powers may be unquestionable as to a particular subject, it is not always easy to determine what their specific duties may be as to the exercise of such powers. They may have power to manage or convey real estate for years or in fee simple, yet the question is left what lands or interests exist for them to control, manage or convey ? They are, therefore, put upon their inquiry to ascertain what there is for them to do or to expend their authority upon, and, in deciding this, they have to consider the manifold rights of private persons, or corporations, to the property about which they propose to act, and as such property is usually real estate, difficult and complicated questions of title or of right continually arise. Concerning much of the property, or of rights claimed by the Town, there are adverse claims by individuals arising out of transactions occurring at one time or another during the past two hundred and twenty years, since the first settlement of the Town. Its claim of title in, and power over, lands under tide waters are apparently in conflict with claims of the State, and of citizens of the State. In fact, all of its claims to lands above or under water are more or less entangled in the web woven by more than two centuries of political, civil and social changes; and can only be determined by exploring the records as far back as any exist; by a study of the charters, grants and patents which are the foundation of its title and by which the Trustees were called into existence and invested with authority; by a careful examination of all laws bearing upon the subject, both during the colonial period and since that time, and an examination of the decisions of the courts, both in England and in this country, construing such charters, grants, patents and laws, in order to discover fully what the language of these documents mean—what is their force and effect, and whether or not the Colonial Governors, who made them had power to do just what they claimed to do; how far they were authorized by the British Sovereign and the Parliament; and how the rights of the Town acquired under them have been affected by subsequent changes in government and legislation.

An historical review of events, material to the subject, since the settlement of the Town to the present time, is essential to the inquiry. Such a review should cover three periods. FIRST.—The period of the Dutch supremacy, down to 1664, the time of the conquest by the English; SECOND.—The period of British Colonial authority, from the above date to the declaration of Independence, 1776; THIRD.—The period covered by the Government of the State of New York from the last mentioned date to the present time.

### THE FIRST OR DUTCH PERIOD.

The Town was first settled under the political authority and domination of the Dutch about 1650, and continued nominally under Dutch rule until 1664, when the British Government seized the country. It was mainly settled by Englishmen who, as the records show, made numerous efforts to annex themselves to the jurisdiction of Connecticut. During this period of about twenty-four years of Dutch rule in Huntington, the inhabitants, who were few in number, made purchases of lands from the native Indians as follows : What is now known as Eaton's Neck was sold by the Indians to Theophilus Eaton, Governor of the Colony of New Haven, in 1646. This was the *first* purchase. There is no existing record of this purchase. In 1653, the first Indian deed was made to the original settlers of Huntington and included about six square miles, running from Cold Spring, on the west, to Great Cow Harbor, now Northport, on the east, and south to the " Old Country Road." This is known as the " *old purchase.*" The deed was given to Richard Holdbrook, Robert Williams and Daniel Whitehead, separate parties, holding separate tracts of the purchase. The consideration given the Indians was six bottles, six coats, six hatchets, six shovels, ten knives, ten fathoms of wampum, thirty eel spears, and thirty needles. It was signed by Assaipune, alias, Mohsua, Sachem of the tribe called Matinecocks. No record of this conveyance can be found and the original has probably been lost.

In 1656, the people of Huntington obtained a deed from the Indians of the country lying between Great Cow Harbor, now Northport, on the west, and the " Nesaquake " River on the east, extending south from the Sound to the " Old Country Road." This is known as the " *Eastern* Purchase." There is no record of this purchase from the Indians now to be found. In 1657, a purchase was made from the Indians by Jonas Wood " and his neighbors " of five necks of meadow lands on the south side of the Town. This purchase seems to have included the Territory lying west of Sumpwams, now Babylon, as far as Great East Neck, and only embraced meadow lands. This deed is on file in the Town Clerk's office, and is the oldest paper in that office of much value. There was also a separate deed made from the Indians to Jonas Wood, during the same year, of the meadows on what was known as " Half Neck," on the south side. In 1658, the Indians deeded to certain of the inhabitants all the meadows west of and including Great East Neck, on the south side, extending beyond the present eastern line of the Town of Oysterbay. No special record of this conveyance can be found, but the fact of this purchase and of the other purchases where no actual record exists, can be established by abundant written evidence scattered through the Town records.

It thus appears, that while under the Dutch jurisdiction, the people, either separately or collectively, had purchased of the Indians a large part of the territory now included within the boundaries of this Town, embracing all of the land lying on the Sound at the north, and on the Great South Bay at the south, excepting a narrow strip of meadow land at Sumpwams, now Babylon. But while holding deeds from the Indians they had not, during this time, done more than taken up and occupied " house lots," principally on what was known as the " Town-spot," the eastern part of the Village of Huntington, enjoying the use of the grass upon the meadows, while such parts of the uplands as had been purchased were held as commons. The records show that the early settlers attached very little value to the uplands, the rule holding good here as everywhere else; that, at the first settlement of a country, the meadow lands along the rivers and margins of the sea and the rich valleys were the first occupied, other lands lying open for common pasturage and the joint use of the people.

During this period of Dutch rule, William Kirft, followed by Peter Stuyvesant, were Governors of the country, and with the aid of a council, exercised all the powers of government; appointed and commissioned all public officers, framed the laws and decided all important controversies. But it appears that as far east as the Town of Huntington the people were permitted to manage, without much interference, their own local affairs in their own way. "The towns in Suffolk County were not subject to the control of any Colony, nor had they any political connection with each other before the conquest, except certain conventional agreements for specific purposes." They elected magistrates and other civil officers whose decisions were appealable to a general town meeting, called the "General Court." No patents were granted nor titles to lands confirmed, by the Dutch Government, to any part of the Territory of Huntington, the people resting their claims solely upon purchases from the Indians and their own occupation. There are very few official records to be found of what occurred during this Dutch period. If there were ever any full records kept of town meetings, or of the doings of public officers, the most of them have been destroyed or lost; and such of them as have survived the waste of time, are either so defaced, or written in such peculiar chirography, that it is almost impossible to decipher their meaning. The oldest paper on file in the Town Clerk's Office, of the Town of Huntington, is dated 1653, and is the record of a Magistrates' Court held in Huntington, at the "Town Spot," now the eastern part of the village. The earliest town meeting of which there remains any record in that office, was held in 1660. From this date to 1664, inclusive, the end of the Dutch period, records exist of the town meetings.

A careful examination of these ancient papers and of contemporaneous history, shows that the early settlers were mainly Englishmen, who, left to their own choice, naturally followed the social, civil and political habits and methods of Englishmen, and of town government, to which they had been accustomed; and in the administration of justice followed the course of the common law rather than the civil law. The only town officers, during this period, seem to have been three overseers, a constable, and several magistrates. The overseers and constable, with the advice of the magistrates, performed all the town business, made and collected rate bills, laid out and maintained highways and watering places, and executed the orders made at town meetings concerning the property held by the proprietors. The people bought and sold land, one of another, under certain restrictions, and a lease of meadow lands was made by the town as early as 1653. But at a town meeting, held in 1662, the following remarkable order was made: "It is this day ordered that no man, possessing house or lands in this Town, shall, at any time, sell, or let, or any way alienate any part of the same to any man or woman, but such as shall be approved of by such men as the Town have chosen for that purpose; only such men as have been freely entered into the Town as inhabitants have the liberty to buy; and whosoever shall break the above-mentioned order shall pay ten pounds to the Town." Jonas Wood, James Chichester, William Leverich and three others were chosen to pass upon all applications by outsiders for a residence in the Town. Usually none, except vicious persons were excluded, and large offers of land were made to induce mechanics and artisans to settle in the Town.

Previous to 1663, it is not probable that there were any official records kept of purchases and sales of land. At a town meeting, held in that year, the following order was made: " Captain Thomas Wicks, Thomas Brush and Isaac Platt are chosen by the Town to take a view of all the lands already laid out in fields, and to record the owner and the quantity he has taken up, in the town book; and, also, these four men have power to dispose of the land into fields or home lots, so as may conduce most to the advantage of those who need lands to improve, and to so lay out as it may not prove prejudicial to the commons, as near as they can to the Town Plot; and to record all such lands so laid out in the town book; and for every acre laid out by these men, the persons employing them are, by the major vote of the Town, appointed to pay sixpence to the acre. "Pursuant to this order, records were made in the town books of the "bounds" of the lands of the inhabitants, at that time, and of such lands as were granted by these individuals, in the name of the Town, to those who hitherto had possessed none. But as the inhabitants were few in number only a small territory was occupied. No conflicts of much importance occurred with the Indians. The lands purchased of them were us. 'ly paid for in wampum, powder and shot, or articles of clothing, and the consideration stated in the deeds is usually trifling in value. There was scarcely any money in the country, and the value at which stock and farm produce passed current was fixed by law. By a vote at a town meeting in 1657, Jonas Holdsworth, an educated Englishman, was employed to teach all the children in the Town, at the Town's expense, his services to be paid for in wampum, Indian corn, and "thriving cattle of ye heifer kind." William Leverich, a missionary, was employed as a minister by the Town, and rate bills levied and collected, with other town charges, for his support. Goodman Chichester, in 1663, was, by vote at a town meeting, given the sole privilege of selling liquor to strangers, and inhabitants were not permitted to buy or sell more than one quart of spirituous liquors at one time. Comparatively few persons could write; most of the deeds or other documents, dating at this period, being attested by a mark. Corporal punishment was commonly inflicted by order of the magistrates. Even women were whipped in the public places for trifling offences. Such an office as Trustee of the Town did not exist during this period.

## THE SECOND, OR BRITISH COLONIAL PERIOD.

In 1664 the country was conquered by the British, and, in pursuance of a grant of territory, including Long Island, by King Charles the Second, to James, Duke of York, made in 1663, Richard Nicoll was appointed Governor of the Colony and took possession of the same. At a general meeting of Deputies from all the Towns on Long Island, held at Hempstead, at which Jonas Wood and John Ketcham represented the Town of Huntington, formal allegiance was rendered to the new government. By the Third Article of the terms of capitulation by the Dutch to the English, it was stipulated that, "all people shall continue free denizens, and shall enjoy their lands, houses, and goods, wheresoever they are, within this country, and dispose of them as they please." The new government was, therefore, bound in honor to uphold and it did maintain all titles or rights respecting lands or goods acquired under the Dutch rule. The purchases from the Indians already made were recognized, but in a code of laws made and promulgated at that date, known as "The Dukes laws," it was declared that "no purchase of lands from the Indians shall be valid without a license from the Governor, and the purchaser shall bring the sachems or right owners before him to confess satisfaction." The want of authority from the Colonial Governors seems to have suspended purchases of lands from the Indians for a long period of years. Immediately after the conquest, in 1664, the purchasers of Indian lands were ordered, by Governor Nicoll, to take out a Patent to confirm their contracts. During the life of King Charles the Second, the Duke of York, as proprietor of the soil, passed many grants, by his Governors, in fee, and after his accession to the throne under the name of James the Second, grants continued to be made under the great seal of the Province, in consequence of the powers given the several Governors by their commissions and instructions from the Crown.

In 1666 the original proprietors of Huntington procured a Patent from Governor Richard Nicoll, by which the whole territory from Cold Spring to Nesaquake River, and from the Sound on the North to the South Sea was erected into a Town. This Patent is now recorded in the office of the Secretary of State at Albany, and a duly certified copy is on file in the Town Clerk's office.

### THE PATENT OF 1666.

This grants "to Jonas Wood, William Leverich, Robert Seely, John Ketcham, Thomas Scidamore, Isaac Platt, Thomas Joanes, and Thomas Weeks, in behalf of themselves, their associates, the freeholders and inhabitants of the Town of Huntington," all the lands which had then been, or thereafter shall be purchased on behalf of the Town from the native proprietors, or others, within the limits therein specified, which boundaries were Cold Spring on the west, running east to Nesaquake River; thence South to the sea; thence west by the sea, including the nine necks of meadow lands on the south side, and all havens, harbors, creeks, meadows," &c., " and all fishing, hawking, hunting," &c., "within the said bounds," " to them, their heirs, successors and assigns forever," " confirming to them all the privileges belonging to a Town within the Government." This grant or Patent gave no right to the Town to purchase other lands, but confirmed their title to such as had already been purchased, or might be afterwards purchased, pursuant to a license from the Colonial Governors.

This Patent embraced within its boundaries what was first known under the name of Caumsett, subsequently as Horse Neck, and now as Lloyd's Manor, or Lloyd's Neck, which territory was, by an Act of the Colonial Legislature, passed in 1691, annexed to Queen's County. It also included all that territory lying between Fresh Pond and Nesaquake River, and which was, in 1694, conveyed to the proprietors of Smithville c. Smithtown, after a protracted and bitter controversy as to title.

The Patent of 1666 conferred no official powers upon the persons named therein. They were not mentioned as Trustees, nor invested with authority to act in behalf of the freeholders and commonalty, in the management and disposal of the Town property, but title was simply confirmed in them, in behalf of the inhabitants.

Under what was called the " Duke's laws," a code of laws promulgated at the time of the Conquest, the shire was divided into three " ridings." Huntington and all east of it being known as the " East Riding." Three grades of Courts were established. The Town or Magistrate's Court ; the Court of Sessions, and the Court of Assizes. Under the Duke's laws and the Patent of 1666 a Town Government was organized ; overseers, constables and magistrates were elected by the people at town meetings, annually held ; overseers laid out and " regulated" highways and watering places, sometimes under express orders made at town meetings, and at other times by virtue of a general authority delegated at town meetings. Very few of these ancient records remain. They also levied and collected the rate bills, and executed orders made at town meeting relating to the Town Government and the management of the common property.

We have seen that previous to the Patent of 1666, grants had been made in open town meetings, of parcels of land usually called " home lots" to individuals, and other grants, or conveyances, had been made, .

of like kind, by persons deputized by the proprietors for that purpose, and records made of the "bounds" thereof, and that these homesteads were near to the "Town Spot," now the eastern part of the Village of Huntington, and the meadow lands not far distant. And we find that for several years after the Patent was given, grants, in like manner, continued to be made. Hitherto, purposes of common defence against the natives, and obedience to that universal law of social commune, which, in the settlement of all new countries, leads the people to dewll near together, the inhabitants had made their dwelling places within comparatively a narrow compass, upon the valleys, meadows and pastures near the sea shore. But now, emboldened by an increase in numbers, and feeling a pressure upon them for more lands, and a wider area of territory for the accommodation of new comers, it was determined to push out into the interior and occupy a new territory. Accordingly, we find that at a town meeting, held Feb. 15, 1872, "It was voted and agreed the same day that the Town should be divided into ten parts, and each part to have a farm and so be engaged to settle them, and every farmer that went forth so to settle, that may be approved of, should enjoy all the remaining parts besides their own, paying all charges and suits of law, or other just charges." That the inhabitants went forth and occupied the lands within the limits of their purchase, as prescribed in the Patent, appears from the numerous records of the period. So fully had the lands been occupied in this way, that in 1675, according to the record in the Town Clerk's Office, there was no more land to grant, but new comers were assured that as soon as further purchases could be made from the Indians all should be supplied. There are no records of any purchases being made from the Indians from the time of the issue of the Patent, in 1666, until 1689. During this period of twenty-three years it appears to have been against the policy of the Colonial Governors to permit purchases from the Indians in this town.

In 1686, Thomas Dongan, then Governor of the Colony, required the inhabitants of the Town to make purchases from the Indians of other territories, and summoned them to appear and show cause by what title they held their lands, in order, as is alleged, that they might be compelled to take out a new Patent. Difficulties arose between him and the Town concerning the payment of the quit-rents, and in that year he seized their Patent of 1666, made them pay his full demands for quit-rents, and issued to them a new Patent. The high handed proceedings of Gov. Dongan, and the procuring of the second Patent, occasioned great commotion in the Town, and was discussed at several town meetings. In 1685, the people voted against giving up the old Patent, but, in 1687, it was agreed to accept a new one upon certain conditions as to what it should contain. The records of this meeting set out those conditions at length, some of which were complied with, and some not. By a vote of the Town, Thomas Powell, Isaac Platt and Capt. Thomas Platt were empowered to negotiate with Governor Dongan, for a new Patent. In the language of the record, "they were left to their liberty in procuring a Patent."

### THE PATENT OF 1688.

This Patent confirmed the title to all lands that had then been purchased, and granted—all lands within the limits of the Town, except five necks of meadow lands at the south, and lands lying north of them remaining unpurchased—absolutely to the inhabitants according to their rights and shares in the original purchase, and regularly incorporated the Town by creating a Board of Public Officers, designated as "THE TRUSTEES OF THE FREEHOLDERS AND COMMONALTY OF THE TOWN OF HUNTINGTON." The Trustees, or Patentees, named in the grant were Thomas Fleet, Sen., Epenetus Platt, Jonas Wood, Sen., James Chichester, Sen., Joseph Baily, Thomas Powell, Sen., John Joanes and Isaac Platt. The grant conveys "all pastures, woods, meadows, marshes, swamps, plains, rivers, rivuletts, waters, lakes, ponds, brooks, streams, beaches, quarries, creeks, harbors, highways, easements, fishing, hawking, hunting and fowling," &c., "with all the rights appurtenant thereto," "to be held in free and common socage according to the manor of East Greenwich, in the County of Kent;" reserving "quit-rent," according to the custom of the period. Full authority is given the Trustees over all the property of the Town, real *and personal*, and "to give, grant, release, alien and assign and dispose of lands, tenements, hereditaments, and every other thing, or things, act and acts, to do and execute by the name aforesaid; to be pleaded and impleaded, defend and be defended in all manner of actions," &c. Perpetuity of the Trustees is created by declaring that "they shall henceforth be elected and *continue to exist forever*." It provides for their making "all rules and orders not repugnant to the laws of England." It required that nine Trustees be annually chosen by the people, in town meeting assembled on the first Tuesday of May. It required to be annually elected one Clerk, one Constable and two Assessors; and provided for the assessment and payment of a yearly rate, or tax, to defray the expenses of the Government, and authorized the Trustees to levy sufficient taxes to defray the charges of the Town.

The Trustees of the Free-Holders and Commonalty of the Town of Huntington, as an official board of public officers, date from this Patent and have their origin in it; and though their number has been diminished, and their powers and duties greatly modified since that time, it is the foundation of their authority. Nevertheless, it does not appear that any Trustees were elected under this Patent. The first Trustees who were ever chosen by the people were elected in 1694, six years afterward. The same Trustees named in the grant continued to act during these six years.

Governor Dongan having given the inhabitants license to purchase of the Indians such lands in the Town as had not hitherto been purchased, we find that very soon after the Patent of 1688 was procured, a large number of deeds were made by the Indians to the whites.

1686, Henry Soper and others purchased of the Indians a tract of land near what is known as "Round Swamp," in this Town.

1689, William Masser purchased of the natives another tract near the same place.

1689, Robert Kellum purchased a tract of land lying at Neguntatogue. ᛕᎬ7ᏟᏔᎾᏔᏔ
1689, Samuel Kisham bought of the natives certain islands of meadow lands lying between the South Meadows and the beach.

1689, Capt. Epenetus Platt, Thomas Weeks, Jonathan Rogers, Nathaniel Foster and all other owners, upon what was known as Santepogue Neck, purchased of the Indians a large tract of upland adjoining their meadows. Imperfect, and in many cases almost unintelligible records of all these deeds, are now in the Town Clerk's Office.

These purchases, made by private persons, were objected to by the people in general, and at a town meeting held the same year it was voted, "That no person purchase lands of the Indians joining the meadows, on the south side, except the inhabitants of East Neck, who may purchase adjoining lands; and further, that no person shall purchase lands of the Indians, within the limits of the Patent, without the consent of the Town, and John Saumis and Samuel Kisham were chosen to purchase lands, generally, of the Indians; and Capt. Platt and Jonas Wood were deputized to purchase the meadows at the South, called Sumpwams, upon the best terms they could make.

Pursuant to these instructions, and otherwise, the following purchases were made:

1689, Sumpwams Neck, at the South, was purchased, including all the meadow lands and the uplands as far north as the "Indian Path," being, in the language of the conveyance, purchased "to the use of the Town of Huntington." There were three separate deeds.

· 1691, Epenetus Platt, Jonas Wood, and their associates, having had license from the Colonial Government and authority from the Town, purchased from the Indians uplands adjoining the meadows on the Neck called Santepogue.

These purchases, since the Patent of 1666, greatly increased the area of common lands, enabled the settlers to improve and occupy new farms and invite and receive into the Town, and accommodate with lands such strangers as were likely to prove advantageous to the common interests, and thus increased very much the population. For several years afterwards the chief business done at town meetings, consisted in making grants of lands to the inhabitants. There seems to have been at this time a general demand for land, and the meadows and uplands were divided and subdivided and surveyed by virtue of orders made by the Trustees, and also by grants made to individuals in open town meeting.

In 1690, it appears that the Patent of 1666—the Nicoll Patent—could not be found, and the people apprehending that their titles and rights might suffer thereby, petitioned the Governor and Council to return them the Patent. This petition is signed by Isaac Platt and Jonas Wood, in behalf of the Town. There is on file in the Town Clerk's Office an original order, certified by Jacob Milburn, Clerk of the Council, directing that the original Patent remain in the Secretary's Office, and that it be recorded in the Town Clerk's Office of the Town of Huntington.

The first election of Trustees was held in April, 1604, as appears by the records of the town meeting, as follows: " At a town meeting legally warned, it was voted and consented unto by the Town, that seven men should be chosen for Trustees for ye management of all Town affairs." "The same day it was voted and consented unto by ye Town that ye seven men ye are chosen Trustees shall have the ordering and management of all Town business; but the Town doth reserve the Patent, if it be within the grant." They were jealous of their rights under the original Patent of Nicoll, and desired to hold to it while conforming to the subsequent grants.

In 1693, it was voted at a town meeting that a further patent be procured from Governor Fletcher, Colonial Governor during the reign of William and Mary ; and they appointed men to procure the same. It was also voted that all who fail to pay their proportion of the expense, have their lands sold at "an outcry."

## THE PATENT OF 1694.

During the following year, 1694, the third Patent was granted by Governor Fletcher, altering the eastern limits of the Town ; confirming all purchases made, and granting all lands, not then purchased of the Indians, within the limits of the Patent, to the Town ; subject, nevertheless, to the Indian claims, where such claims had not been extinguished by purchase, or otherwise. The corporate limits of the Town were by this Patent very much abridged. As we have seen, Lloyd's Neck had been set off to Queens County and erected into a Manor; and a survey of the line between Huntington and the Town of Oyster Bay made in 1684, had placed the westernmost of the Necks on the South side, once claimed by Huntington, into Oyster Bay. On the East, Huntington lost all the country lying between Fresh Pond and the Nesequake river. Under this Patent seven Trustees were named; and it was declared that the acts and orders of the Trustees should be certified "by a common seal, affixed thereto," and " signed by the President of the Trustees, who is first to be chosen of the said Trustees." Full power is confirmed and given to the Trustees, in this Patent, to take, hold, manage and dispose of all and every kind of property, for and in behalf of the Town. After reciting the substance of former Patents, this proceeds to affirm " that Joseph Bayly, and six others, in behalf of themselves and the inhabitants of Huntington, have by petition prayed a grant and confirmation of the premises, so only that the limits and boundaries of the Town of Huntington shall not be as above mentioned, but as thereafter specified ; that is to say : all these tracts and necks of land, lying (upon Long Island), on our Island of Nassau, within our County of Suffolk, being bounded on the west by a river called and known by the name of Cold Spring, and running south from the head of the said Cold Spring to the South Sea; and on the north by the Sound that runs between our said Island of Nassau and the main Continent ; upon the east by a line running from the east side of a Pond, called and known as the Fresh Pond, to the west side of Whitman's Dale, or Hollow, and thence to a river on the south side of our said Island of Nassau, on the east side of a neck called Sumpwams, and from the said River, running south to the South Sea. And, whereas, we would be greatly pleased to make, erect, and establish all our loving subjects, the inhabitants and freeholders in our said Town of Huntington, within the limits and bounds next above expressed, into our body politique and corporate, in deed and name, when reasonably requested, being willing to grant : Now know ye that of our special grace, certain knowledge, and motion ; we have given, granted," &c., " to Joseph Bayly," and others named, " all of the aforesaid tracts and Necks of land." (Here follows the same description given last above,) "together with all the houses, messuages, tenements, buildings, mills, mill-dams, gardens, orchards, fields, pastures, feedings, woods, underwoods, trees, timber, common of pasture, meadows, marshes, swamps, plains, rivers, rivulets, waters, lakes, ponds, brooks, streams, heaths, quarries, streets, harbors, highways and easements, fishing, fowling, hunting and hawking, mines, minerals, (silver and gold mines excepted) and all other franchises, profits, appertaining," &c., " within the limits and bounds next above mentioned."

After the Patent of 1694 was given by Governor Fletcher, other purchases were made from the Indians as follows:

At a Town meeting held in 1696, the Trustees were authorized to purchase of the Indians lands near *Massepage*, and in pursuance of this in the year

1697, Josiah's Neck, South, and neighboring Territory, were purchased and became the property of the Town.

Hitherto all deeds of land by the Indians to the inhabitants had been made, either to individuals for their own benefit, or to be by the grantees divided up into allotments in behalf of all the proprietors; but in the year

1700 we, for the first time, find a deed made by the natives directly to the Town in its corporate capacity. This is a conveyance to John Weeks, John Wood, Epenetus Platt, Ensign Jarvis, Richard Brush, and John Ketcham, present Trustees of the Freeholders and Commonalty of the Town of Huntington, of a tract of land north of the " Indian Path;" south, adjoining the purchases already made for the Town.

1700. Jonas Wood bought of the Indians for the Town, pursuant to the authority already referred to, Little East Neck, or the uplands adjoining it.

1702. The Indians conveyed to the Trustees of the Freeholders and Commonalty of the Town of Huntington other uplands, adjoining Sumpwams, south.

1703. Jonas Wood purchased of the natives certain meadows of East Neck, south, and uplands. This seems to have been a private purchase, made in conformity to the authority given by the Town, before referred to.

1705. The Indians conveyed to the Town, through its Trustees, " a parcel of land on ye west side of Masapogue Gut, bounded on ye south by ye ocean sea, and ye north by ye Sound, with all sunken marshes and islands," &c., a very indefinite boundary.

1705. A purchase was made by the Trustees of the lands known as Neguntatogue, bounded on the south by the meadows formerly purchased of the Indians ; north, by two swamps ; west, by the river, and on the east by the Santepogue river. The original deed, as executed by the Indians, is now on file in the Town Clerk's Office, as also is the deed of Sumpwams.

The several purchases from the Indians heretofore cited, being fifteen in number, probably embrace about all that were ever made. Such as were made after the Fletcher Patent were made under licenses from the Governors of the Province, regulated in a measure by the voice of the people in town meeting assembled.

In addition to these conveyances by the native Indians and their confirmation, and the charters and grants from the Crown of England, we have the sanction and ratification of the same by the legislative power of the Colony ; and also confirming all that had lawfully been done by virtue thereof, notwithstanding any omission or irregularity in the manner of exercising or enjoying the rights thereby confirmed. By this Act, passed in 1691, it was enacted, "that all the charters, patents and grants authorized, made, given and granted," &c., "by their late and present Majesties, the Kings of England," &c., unto the several corporations, and bodies politick of the cities, towns or manors, and also of the several and respective freeholders within this Province, are, and forever shall be, esteemed and reputed good and effective charters, patents, and grants, authentick in the law against their Majesties, their heirs or successors forever, notwithstanding of the want of form in the law, or the nonfeazance of any right, privilege, or custom, which ought to have been done heretofore by the constitutions and directions contained in the respective charters, patents and grants aforesaid." It was further enacted that the grantees should "have, hold, exercise, occupy, possess and enjoy all their rights, customs, prerogatives, privileges, preheminencies, practices, immunities, liberties, franchises, royalties and usages, whatsoever, in as full and ample a manner as if none of these changes, alterations, disturbances, want of other forms in the law or the nonfeazance of any rights, privileges or customs, of any of the corporations aforesaid, had never happened or been neglected."

It was also enacted by the Colonial Assembly in 1691 : " That the freeholders in every respective town within this Province are hereby empowered and authorized to meet and assemble themselves together at such times and places as are appointed, and expressed in their respective grants and patents, and when so assembled to make, establish, constitute and ordain, from time to time, such prudential orders and rules for the better improving of their respective lands in tillage, pasturage, or any other reasonable way, as shall by the majority of freeholders, so assembled or convened as aforesaid, be thought good and convenient." Another section of the same act authorizes the election of three surveyors, who, pursuant to orders made at town meetings, were empowered to "lay out, set forth, regulate and amend," all highways and fences. Subsequently, power was given to establish and maintain public watering places ; and all highways and watering places were required to be recorded in the Town Clerk's Office.

From the date of the last Patent, 1694 to 1776, the end of the Colonial period, covering a space of eighty-two years, the records of the Town though in a worn and tattered condition, are tolerably complete as to these matters of title to lands which come more particularly within the purpose of this inquiry. The limits of the Town, with respect to its juris-diction in civil and criminal matters, remained the same as established by the last Patent. The title of the Indians, such as it was, gradually gave way to purchase by the whites, their death or removal to other localities; and thus a perfect title became vested in the Town, in its corporate capacity, of all lands not already allotted to the inhabitants; and the titles of the latter were fully ratified and confirmed.

The manner in which the original proprietors divided the land is involved in some obscurity. As they paid the Indians very little for an extinguishment of their title, and paid the Colonial Governments no more for the title acquired under the Patents, than certain small sums for. drafting the instruments (aside from a quit-rent, which was only nominal), their lands cost them very little. Nevertheless, these expen-ditures were the real consideration for the land, and each proprietor held according to the proportion of this consideration paid by him. Those who failed to pay their share had their lands, or rights, sold at an "outcry." In process of time the original consideration gave place to an increased valuation, and the rights of the ancient proprietors were held as hundred pound rights, or more, as the case might be. At town meetings held in 1724-25-30, a division was made in each of the years mentioned, of ten acres to a hundred right in the "old purchase;" and by order of the Trustees in 1723 a division of twenty acres to the hundred was made in the "eastern purchase." From 1696 to 1762, there are voluminous records of surveys "to the right" of individuals named, usually in small parcels, and made by order of the Trustees of the Town. The various modes therefore by which title has passed to individuals are:

*First*, grants by the ancient proprietors in open town meeting.

*Second*, grants, or conveyances, made by the agents of the proprie-tors, duly authorized to make such conveyances by the "major vote" at town meetings.

*Third*, conveyances by order of the Trustees, pursuant to orders made at town meetings, without any corporate seal or acknowledge-ments.

*Fourth*, conveyances by the Trustees in their corporate capacity, evidenced by their corporate seal, and executed in the usual manner, pursuant to the patents and laws.

Though the people of the Town had, by an order made at a town meeting as early as 1663, provided for recording in the "Town Book," the "bounds" of lands, held or conveyed by the inhabitants, it was not until 1710 that the Colonial Assembly prescribed a certain mode of record. In that year there was passed: "An Act for the better settlement and assurance of lands in this Colony." By the fourth section it was enacted as follows:

"Whereas by many accidents the deeds and writings relating to estates, sometime have been, and hereafter may be, destroyed, consumed and lost, whereby the lawful and rightful owner of any lands, messuages, houses, tenements and hereditaments, may be exposed to many doubtful, expensive and vexatious suits, and other inconveniences, for the preventing whereof; Be it enacted by the authority, aforesaid, that all and every deed, or deeds, conveyance, or conveyances, and writings relating to the title or property of any lands, messuages, tenements, or hereditaments, within this Colony, which have been already, or hereafter shall be, executed, being duly acknowledged and recorded in the Secretarie's Office of the said Colony, or in the County records, where such lands are situate, and being such deed or writing, so recorded, or transcript hereof, shall be good and effectual evidence in any court of record within this Colony, to all intents and purposes, as if the original deed, or deeds, conveyance, or conveyances, and writings, was or were produced and proved in court.

Eminent counsel have considered that a grave question may arise as to the validity of some of these conveyances, or informal allotments and divisions, made by authority of town meetings, or officers empowered by them. They have not been able to satisfactorily solve the problem as to how lands, held in common by the ancient proprietors, have become legally vested in individuals, without the formalities and solemnities of a deed, under seal, in conformity to the statute of frauds. No case, it is believed, has hitherto arisen which has given an opportunity for adjudicating this point. It seems that the most reasonable ground upon which such conveyances can be upheld, is that of *partition by consent*, and the legal effects of such partition. Perhaps the defect of title, if such, was in part cured by an act of the "Colonial Assembly," passed in 1726, the title of which was as follows; "An Act for the easier partition of lands held in common and for promoting the settling and improvement thereof; and for *confirming divisions in the settled Townships of this Colony*." The difficulty would seem to be overcome by the various acts for quieting title, passed by the Colonial and State Legislatures, the first of which was passed in 1710, and confirmed the title to all persons in possession from the year 1700 to 1713, without adverse claim, evidenced by entry or suit brought to recover. In view of the lapse of time and the multitude of ways in which these titles have been recognized, we think it hardly any longer a living issue.

The Trustees, by virtue of the authority vested in them by the grants, and patents, and laws, continued to hold, manage and dispose of the property of the Town. At first they had authority for, and did lay out and maintain highways and watering places, and regulated the same. Subsequently, the Colonial Assembly vested this power in three Surveyors, annually chosen, acting under orders of town meetings. Still later, the office of Commissioner of Highways was created, and all the official authority of Trustees over highways and public easements generally, ceased.

They sold and conveyed common lands of the Town to individuals and corporations, both interior lands and lands bordering upon the shores of tide waters; and in some cases they conveyed to individuals the lands under the tide waters of the harbors and bays, in fee, for dock purposes, or on account of its value in yielding an annual growth of salt grass. They leased lands under tide-waters, above and below low water mark, for wharf purposes, and prescribed rules and regulations for the use of such property, reserving a nominal rent, but watching with jealous care the maintenance of the rights of the Town over this species of property. In 1765-74, and, probably at other times, they leased to individuals the whole of the South Bay. They also leased the undivided common lands in the interior of the island, giving the lessee the right to cut and carry away wood and timber, at a nominal rent. In 1764, they leased to Jonathan Titus the exclusive right to run a ferry between Huntington and Norwalk, in Connecticut, for a period of five years, at a rent of sixteen pounds each year, requiring the lessee to give bonds to the amount of 200 pounds, that a good ferry should be maintained. They continued to lease this ferry for many years.

At an early period, the Town owned a grist mill at Cowharbor. This property was managed by the Trustees, and finally sold. At different periods suits were instituted against parties for carrying away stone (for paving purposes) from the shores of the harbors and bays on the Sound, within what was believed to be the limits of the Town. They made many regulations and orders, dating back to a very early period, against non-residents hunting or fishing within the limits of the Town. These orders were especially directed against the taking and carrying away of oysters and other shell-fish by non-residents.

Under the Colonial laws, the Trustees were invested with authority in the matter of establishing and maintaining a church. They were the legal holders and managers of the church property, both as to the church buildings and the parsonage lands, which were, at an early day, set off to the church and located on West-Neck. In 1717, the oldest church in the Town, located on a stream of water near the "Town Spot," was sold for five pounds, by a vote of the people at a town meeting, and another erected a little further east, by the Trustees, mainly with funds raised by a tax on the whole Town. The minister was paid by a rate bill on the whole Town. Tho Trustees directed as to who might occupy seats in the church, and a Constable was, by a vote of the town meeting, assigned the duty of compelling our worthy ancestors to preserve proper order and decorum within the sanctuary, and, at the same time, to prevent any of " ye horses, oxen or swine frequenting ye highways within one mile of the church." But authority in church matters has long since departed from the Trustees in so far as it appertained to their official capacity.

The difficulties and conflict of title that arose between the Town and the proprietors of what was known as the " Bating Place Purchase," and which were adjusted by referees in 1704; and the suits between the claimants under the "Squawpit Purchase," are not material to this inquiry, as they have long since been settled, and the rights of the town fully determined.

#### THE PERIOD OF THE GOVERNMENT OF THE STATE OF NEW YORK.

Obedient to the general principle, that where the political power is changed, either by conquest or successful revolution, the internal laws and customs of a people remain in force until changed or abrogated by the new sovereignty, very many of the old Colonial laws continued to have force after the declaration of independence in 1776, and the organization of a State government. The title which the people had acquired to property, and, especially, their rights and franchises under the old charters, grants and patents, were fully protected and maintained. By the first Constitution of the State of New York, and also by the Constitution of 1821, and by the Constitution of 1846, now in force, it is provided that nothing therein contained shall affect any grants of land within this State, made by the authority of the King of Great Britain, or his predecessors; or shall annul any Charters to bodies' politic or corporate, by him or them made, before October 14, 1775. (See Article I, Sec. 18, Constitution.)

By the thirty-fifth Article of the Constitution of 1777, it was ordained " that such parts of the common law of England, and of the statutes of England, and of Great Britain, and of the Acts of the Legislature of the Colony of New York as together did form the law of the said Colony on the 19th day of April, 1775, shall be and constitute the law of the State, subject to such alterations and provisions as the Legislature of this State, from time to time, may make concerning the same." The subsequent constitutions ordain the same in substance. Thus the validity of the grants to the Town of Huntington are recognized and acknowledged by the fundamental law of the State of New York.

By an Act of the Legislature of this State, passed in 1784, it was enacted "that from and after the passage of this Act it shall and may be lawful to and for the freeholders and inhabitants of the Town of Huntington, to hold their annual town meeting on the first Tuesday in April, in each year, and on no other day," and then elect Trustees, a Supervisor, Town Clerk, Assessors, Constables, Overseers of the Poor, Overseers of the Highways, and Fence Viewers;" and, also, "at such annual town meetings to make such rules and regulations respecting the Town, and to transact all such business, in the same manner as it was lawful for them to do at their annual town meetings heretofore." Though by the language of the twenty-ninth Article of the Constitution of 1777, it was inferred that Trustees should be elected by the People, the above is the first formal enactment by the legislature of the State that, they should be so elected. The Patent of 1688 required their annual election, but, as we have seen, it was not until six years thereafter, 1694, that any Trustees were elected by the People, those appointed in and by the grant of 1688 continuing to hold office.

By an Act of the Legislature of the State, passed in 1788, it was declared "that it may be lawful for the freeholders of each and every of the said Towns, at any of their Town meetings, to direct money to be raised for prosecuting or defending the common rights of such Town, as the major part of such Freeholders and inhabitants so assembled, shall deem necessary and proper." The fifth Section of the Act of 1823 declares: "that the people when so assembled may make rules for directing the use and management, and the times and the manner of using their common lands and meadows, and the other commons."

This only re-enacted in this respect what had always been the law since the first settlement of the Town by force of State and Colonial laws and custom.

These Constitutional ordinances and Acts of the Legislature have been quoted and referred to in order to understand the situation, and to be able to measure the powers of the Trustees, so far as the letter of the law is concerned. These powers would seem to be ample for all purposes of protecting the rights of the people of the Town in their common property and the holding, managing or conveying thereof. But the question still remains: what common property is left for them to manage? What are the limits of the Town within which the Trustees can lawfully exercise their powers? During the past two hundred years the wide extent of common lands, once held, has been divided and conveyed to individuals and corporations, and there are only left the meadows on certain necks and islands at the south; a limited quantity of marsh lands on the north side, and here and there a few parcels of upland. Independent of these the Town claim lands under the tide-waters that wash its northern and southern shores. The right of the Town to lease, or sell, such lands under water, and give a valid title therefor; and the particular localities over which that authority extends, remain to be considered, in the light which the charters, patents, grants, deeds, Colonial laws, Constitutions, Statutes, and decisions of the Courts shall throw upon the subject.

Numerous controversies have arisen between the Town of Huntington and adjoining towns as to the lawful boundaries of the Town. Smithtown, Islip and Oysterbay, have successively encroached upon our boundaries, as claimed and set forth in the Patents; and in all these controversies, Huntington has been unsuccessful. Lloyd's Neck was wrested from the Town by an Act of the Colonial Legislature in 1691, upon the ground, mainly, that the territory had been purchased from the Indians by three residents of Oysterbay, prior to the Patent of 1666; and, therefore, belonged to the jurisdiction of Oysterbay. Again the controversy with Oysterbay concerning the westermost of the three Necks purchased from the Indians by authority of the Town of Huntington on the south bay, was determined adversely to Huntington by the Governor and Assembly of Deputies, convened to decide the dispute at Hempstead, notwithstanding, it was admitted by the order of determination that Huntington had the best right to the territory. Beside these, long and severely contested litigations existed, at different periods, between Huntington and Oysterbay, concerning the true line of division; they were settled in various ways, and the lines surveyed and monuments established by commissions; first in 1684; second in 1734; third in 1797; and the fourth time in 1800, and are now well understood, except as to the line opposite East Beach and the eastermost part of Lloyd's Neck, the survey having terminated opposite the point of the above Beach; leaving the line of the jurisdiction of the respective towns undetermined to the north of that point. We think, however, that Oysterbay can only claim to high-water mark on Huntington Bay. The dispute with Smithtown as to the line has already been alluded to, and, we have seen, that Huntington in 1694 lost all the territory lying between the Fresh Pond and Nesaquake River, and a part of the territory claimed as within Winnecomac Patent; but the line is now defined with certainty. A long and bitter litigation took place between Huntington and the Nicoll family of Islip, as to the ownership of *Cup Tree*, Cedar and Grass Islands, in the South Bay. The boundaries between Huntington and Islip are adjusted.

But while the boundaries of the Town are defined by distinct marks and monuments on the east and west, the exact limits on the north and south, over which its Trustees may lawfully exercise ownership, absolute or qualified, remain *undetermined* by any lines established by law. These limits are only to be ascertained by reference to judicial decisions, or the general principles controling the interpretation of the charters and grants, as to the extent to which title is conferred, running into and under the ebb and flow of salt water. The vital question is, where is the boundary established by the patents? What territory did the King, through his Colonial Governors, undertake to, and succeed in vesting in the Town of Huntington by these grants?

### THE RIGHTS OF THE TOWN IN LANDS UNDER TIDE WATERS.

Preliminary to a deeper inquiry into the origin and nature of the title claimed by the Town, it is proper to state here that the Town has always claimed title in the soil under the tide waters of such creeks, coves, harbors, bays, and havens, as lie adjacent to its uplands, and an exclusive right *in the inhabitants of the Town* to appropriate the oysters and other shell-fish growing in such waters. That it has always claimed the exclusive right, within such territory, to lease or dispose of such lands for the cultivation of oysters, for dock and other purposes, subject to the common right of navigation. There is good reason to believe that the Town has exercised those rights during the past *two hundred years.* Our ancestors were accustomed to declare and order, when assembled in town meeting, "That if any person that doth not belong to the township shall hunt, hawk, fowl, or fish, within this Township, he shall be prosecuted for the same, and damages recovered before a Justice of the Peace." More than fifty orders similar to the above are recorded in the town records. Between 1691 and 1759, the Colonial Legislature passed numerous laws regulating the oyster-fisheries, and especially prohibiting all non-residents of the Colony from taking shell-fish from its waters, establishing penalties for violation of the same. This prohibition against non-residents has never ceased to have force. The Town has, during the same period, and does now, hire out, sell, and lease, the thatch-beds and salt grass upon the margin of, and extending into, and under the flow of, salt water, comprising the creeks, harbors, bays, &c., on the north and south sides of the Town. The grants and laws herein referred to were supposed to confer such authority upon the Trustees, and furnish them with all needful remedies against any and all invasion of the rights of the Town in the premises.

We come now to the main question: Has the town title in lands under tide waters? If so, where is the outermost limit of such title? and what is the nature of that title? The public statutes describe the boundaries of the Town as follows: "The Town of Huntington shall contain all that part of said County (Suffolk) called and known by the name of Huntington, including Eaton's Neck and Crab Meadow."

With respect to tide waters, an important distinction exists between the limits of the territorial jurisdiction of a town within which, upon the one hand, it may exercise political powers—the administration of the laws civil and criminal—and on the other hand, lawfully claim title to lands under such waters, and exercise exclusive privileges therein. We believe it is not disputed that the territorial jurisdiction of the State of New York extends to the middle of Long Island Sound. Upon the principle that the several towns in the State embrace every part of its territory, the northern boundary of the Town of Huntington must be coextensive with that of the State, and run to the middle of the Sound, along its entire northern boundary. Upon the south it borders on the ocean, and upon well settled principles of law the jurisdiction of the State extends a marine league, or three miles, into the sea from the shore. The jurisdiction of the Town will therefore extend to the same line along its entire southern boundary. But this wide extent of jurisdiction over the sea and the Sound is in part confined, in its nature, to the administration of the laws; is a political jurisdiction, and does not necessarily carry with it a title to the soil under the waters, or an exclusive ownership in the products of the Sound or sea within such boundaries. In the absence of all grants, derived from or under the King of Great Britain, or the Legislature of the State of New York, the State would own the soil, subject to certain qualifications, under tide waters everywhere below high water mark. It remains to be seen how far the State stands divested of these rights, and the Town has become invested, by means of the several grants upon which the claim of the latter is based.

As the town necessarily traces its title back to a period anterior to the existence of the present Government of the State of New York, and directly to the Government of Great Britain, through its charters and grants, we must measure the force and effect of these instruments, and all the circumstances connected with them, by the laws and usages of England, in force at the time, and subsequent to that time. As we trace title to the King of England, we must see by what tenure he held, what he had power to grant, and what he did grant. Purchases from the Indian Natives, as of their aboriginal right, were never held to be a valid, legal title in the Province of New York, unless confirmed by the Crown. Conveyances by the Indians to the original settlers simply extinguished the Indian right of occupation, but did not carry title to the soil. All Indian rights in the Town have long since been extinguished by their conveyances, their death, or removal.

The Government of Great Britain claimed its territories in America by virtue of the right of discovery. (A legal fiction which it is now quite too late to controvert). Its subjects, when they landed on these shores, took possession in the name of the King of England, and held under the authority of that Government. Hence the King, as the representative of British sovereignty, became the source of all titles to lands embraced within the discovered territories. The Supreme Court of the United States very clearly stated this doctrine in the case of *Johnson vs. McIntosh*, (8 Wheaton, 595). The Court says: "According to the theory of the British Constitution all vacant lands are vested in the Crown as representing the Nation, and the exclusive power to grant them is admitted to reside in the Crown, as a branch of the royal prerogative." The common law of England vests in the King the title to all public property, and this title includes, as well the rivers and seas as the dry lands, within the territorial limits.

In the case of the *Attorney-General vs. Richards*, in the Exchequer, the information stated that "by the royal prerogative the sea, and the sea-coasts, and as far as the sea flows and reflows, between the high and the low water-mark, and all the ports and havens of the Kingdom belong to his Majesty," &c. Angell in his excellent treatise on Tide-waters, page 20, says: "The right of property in tide-waters in England is moreover vested in the King, not merely on the principle that he is the universal occupant, but on the principle of his being the fountain from whence, in contemplation of law, all authority and privilege proceed; to the King of England is therefore not only assigned the sovereign dominion of the sea adjoining the coasts, and over the arms of the sea, but in him is also vested 'the right of property in the soil thereof."

At the time of the revolution, in 1776, the people of this country took into their own hands the sovereignty which had hitherto been lodged in the Crown, and deposited the same in the several States. By virtue of the revolution the State of New York came to stand in the place of the King, as to all property within its territories. An Act passed by the Legislature of the State of New York in 1779, expresses this radical change in the following language: "That the absolute property of all messuages, lands, tenements, and hereditaments, and of all rents, royalties, franchises, prerogatives, privileges, escheats, forfeitures, debts, dues, duties, and services of whatsoever names respectively, the same are called and known in the law; and all right and title to the same, which next and immediately before the ninth day of July, in the year of our Lord, one thousand seven hundred and seventy-six, did vest in, or belong, or was, or were due to the Crown of Great Britain, be, and the same and each, and every of them, hereby are declared to be, and ever since the said ninth day of July, in the year of our Lord, one thousand seven hundred and seventy-six, to have been, and forever hereafter shall be vested in the people of this State, in whom the sovereignty and seignority thereof are and were united and vested on and from the said ninth day of July," &c.

As to lands already granted, whether above or below tide waters, though the State might, by virtue of its sovereignty, in a measure control the manner of their use, and in the exercise of the trust it held, protect all public rights therein, it could not, nor did it seek to abrogate the titles already granted by the British Government; but it is bound to, and does, protect all persons or corporations in the enjoyment of the ownership thus previously acquired. The quotations heretofore made from the Constitutions and Statutes of the State of New York, fully support this position. On the other hand, all lands, above or under tide waters, which had not, previous to the revolution, been alienated by the Crown, were, by virtue thereof, vested in the State, to be by the State, in the exercise of its sovereignty, controlled, managed, or disposed of, in such manner as the legislative power might direct.

The Town of Huntington claims ownership of the soil under tide waters by virtue of the several charters, patents and grants, coming mediately or immediately from the Crown of England; and to the extent which is embraced in such grants, the soil is not, and never was owned by the State of New York; but the grantees in the patents, and all claiming under them, are invested with a valid title thereto. This brings us to the consideration of the nature and extent of the ownership of the Town to lands under tide waters, based on a proper construction of the charters and patents.

The force and effect of the Charter given by Charles the Second, to the Duke of York, under which the first patent, that of 1666, was granted, has been adjudicated upon in the State Courts, and in the Supreme Court of the United States. Without going into the question whether this Charter was exclusively a grant of political power by the King, for the sole purpose of organizing, carrying on and maintaining a government in America, or whether, in addition to this, it carried from the King to the Duke a private title in the soil; (a question upon which authorities differ,) we think it may be safely affirmed, and that without running counter to the decision in *Martin vs. Waddell* (16 Peter's U. S. R., 369), that after the Colonial Government had been organized and clothed with all the powers of a government, executive, judicial and legislative, it had power under the Charter to grant title in the name and in behalf of the King, to lands within the boundaries therein prescribed. And though, with respect to lands under tide waters, the Duke of York stood in the place of the King, holding them in trust for all the people, he might grant title therefor, and especially when his grant was ratified by the legislative power of the Colony, as we have seen was done in this case, thereby receiving the sanction of the whole political power controlling the particular subject, and competent to vest in the Town of Huntington, a valid title to whatever lands, above or under water, came properly within the terms of his Charter.

The first patent, given by Governor Nicoll, in 1666, was under authority of the above charter, and was strictly a grant of land, conveying title within specified boundaries, as follows: "From a certain river, or creek, on the west, commonly called by the Indians by the name of Nackaquatck, and by the English the Cold Spring, to stretch Eastward to Nasaquake river; on the north to be bounded *by ye Sound, running betwixt Long Island and the Maine*, and on ye south by ye sea," &c., "with all havens, harbors, creeks, waters," &c.

In private grants by the King, arms of the sea are excluded, but in grants, which, in addition to conveying the soil, carry political powers, arms of the sea are included. *Angell on Tide Waters, page 38*, says: "But inasmuch as the King, by virtue of his prerogative, was authorized to create *political power* in this, as in all countries newly discovered and possessed by his subjects, the colonies, on receiving the royal charters, were invested with a *political character* by which they succeeded to the territorial interests which had previously belonged, as *jure regalia*, to the sovereign power of the parent country. These charters were in the nature of *grants*, and were conferred by the King on this idea, that he was proprietor. But as they respectively created governments, it is to be observed they were not construed as his other grants were; that is as not excluding arms of the sea, but as including them. And it was thus that the several colonies were invested with the sovereign authority, delegated by the Crown, to alter the common law in respect to their tide waters, or to grant an exclusive property therein at their discretion."

When the Duke of York, through his Governor, Nicoll, in 1666, granted to certain inhabitants of Huntington the territory before mentioned, and expressly granted therein that they, their heirs, and assigns, shall have "all the privileges of a town government within this government;" he conferred on them political powers, and by using the same comprehensive terms that the charter contained, doubtless intended to make the grant as broad as the language indicates, and thus include "all havens, harbors, bays, creeks, and rivers," &c., with "all fishing, hawking, hunting," &c., embracing *all arms of the sea* within the prescribed boundaries. As we have already seen, twenty-two years after the first patent, when the Duke of York had become King of England, he, as King, through his then Colonial Governor, Thomas Dongan, made a new grant confirming the former grant, at the same time granting other lands, and enlarging the powers of the Town Government. The water boundaries remained as in the former grant. This patent was approved by the Council of the Colony of New York, and was afterwards confirmed by the Colonial Assembly. It was a grant of soil, using the unmistakable words, "give, grant, bargain, sell, alienate."

It also carried with it political power commensurate with the purposes of a town government, taking it out of the rule that a private grant of soil to a subject is to be construed against the subject, and in favor of the King, and bringing it within that other rule, that where a grant carries political power it shall be construed in favor of the grantee. If there is any reasonable doubt about the power of the Duke of York, to grant titles to the soil by virtue of this charter from Charles the Second, all difficulty is obviated upon that point by his having made this second grant through Governor Dongan, after he himself had become King of England.

Seven years after the second grant was made, as appears in the preceding pages, a third patent was given by Governor Fletcher, in the name of William and Mary, representing the Crown of England. This confirms all former grants, and changes the eastern boundaries, but does not affect its northern or southern limits under tide waters. The language is, as to the northern boundary, "The Sound that runs between our said Island of Nassau and the main Continent," while the "Sea" is designated as the southern boundary, including "all havens, harbors, creeks, coves, rivers," &c., and "all fishing, hunting," &c., within the before-mentioned boundaries.

We may be aided in arriving at a proper construction of these patents by a reference to the principles of construction admitted by the English Courts.

In *The King against the Bishop of Rochester and Sir Francis Clarke;* Hilary Term, (24, E. 25, Car. 2, Roll. 504), Hurders, Sergeant, laid down four grounds or rules whereby to construe the King's Letters Patent:

*First.*—When a particular certainty precedes, it shall not be destroyed by an uncertainty coming after.

*Second.*—There is a difference when the King mistakes his title to the prejudice of his tenure or profit, and when he is mistaken only in some description of his grant, which is but supplemental and not material, nor issuable.

*Third.*—Distinct words of relation in the King's grant are good to pass away anything.

*Fourth.*—When the King's grants are upon a valuable consideration they shall be construed favorable for the patentee, for the honor of the King. The Court rendered judgment upon these principles. 1 Mod., p. 75.

In the *King vs. Bishop of Chester:* "Where a grant of the King may be taken to two intents, one good and the other not, it shall be construed to such intent as makes the grant good." "Where his intention appears to pass the thing, it shall pass." 4. Mod., p. 301.

The case of *Lowndes vs. Dickerson*, tried at the Suffolk County Circuit, and affirmed on appeal to General Term, 34 Barb. 580, is relied on by those who oppose the title of the Town and its rights over the fisheries. Lowndes and others planted oysters in what the Court called "Northport Bay," where from the evidence, it appears there was no natural growth of oysters; they were non-residents of the Town, but citizens of the State. Dickerson, a resident of the Town of Huntington, took and carried away oysters from the bed thus planted. In a suit for trespass by Lowndes and others, plaintiffs recovered. We think the issues were not such as could fairly test the rights of the Town. The Court decided the case on one ground, viz.: that the premises were not within the boundaries of the Town of Huntington under its Patents.

The question whether the King had a right to grant an exclusive fishery to the inhabitants of Huntington or not, did not enter into or form any part of the grounds upon which this case was determined, for the good reason that if the premises in question were not within the grant, it was a matter of no consequence what was the force and effect of the patents as to granting an exclusive fishery within its boundaries. Therefore the intimations of the learned Judge Brown, who decided that case adversely to the power of the King to grant an exclusive fishery, are simply *obiter dicta* and have no judicial force. We have reason to believe the facts were not all before the Court, bearing upon the point, upon which the case terminated so adverse to the interests of the Town. The evidence seems to have been deficient with respect to the geographical character of the locality, judging from the language of the Court, who said, "The argument of the defendant proceeds upon the theory that there are no harbors, havens or creeks inside of the south shore of the Sound upon the rivers or inlets, if any, which intersect the Island, in the Town of Huntington, to which the words quoted (in the Patent), can apply. *The proof is silent in respect thereto.*" It is unfortunate for the Town that the proof should have been silent upon so important a point.

In this case the Court affirm the principle: "A grant bounded upon a navigable river, that is a river flowed by the tide, extends to the edge of the water only." The edge of the water, here referred to, must necessarily extend as far inland as the water on the creek, or stream, is affected by the flow and reflow of the tide. If, as in this case declared, this "edge of the water" is the boundary of the Town, such a construction is inconsistent with the express language of the grants to the Town, which declare, after given the Sound as the northern boundary, that the granted territory shall include all havens, bays, harbors, creeks, rivers, &c. The manner in which the learned Judge reconciles this inconsistency is, to say the least, ingenious. He says : " But there is an express limitation upon the effect of these words, (havens, harbors, &c.,) in the Patent itself, which declares that the havens, harbors, creeks, &c., with the other rights and franchises, are to be ' within the limits and bounds next above mentioned '; that is they are such as may be within the limits of the territory bounded north by the shores of Long Island Sound,"

As under the construction, above given, this *shore* of Long Island Sound extends as far inland as the tide sensibly affects the creeks and streams that run into the Sound, we are at a loss to understand where, under any possible conditions, any harbors, bays, havens, &c., can be found in this Town. To say that the grant shall go to the edge of the water, " together with all harbers, havens," &c., " within the bounds above mentioned ;" is as absurd as to have included, among the other properties set forth with such care, all ships and vessels sailing on dry land, above the edge of the water or shore. But it seems " the proof was silent " upon this point, whether there were any such harbors, havens, &c.

When the Court affirms that the grant is bounded by the shores of Long Island Sound, and locates these shores inside of all the harbors, havens, creeks, and rivers, as far as the tide ebbs and flows, it does violence to the language of the Patent ; that language is : bounded " by Long Island Sound " ; not the *shores* of the Sound. The term " *shore*" is judicially defined to include all that space between high and low water-mark ; a space of very considerable extent in the shallow waters of harbors, coves and creeks. Treatise De Jure Maris & Hall on the rights to the sea; Cortelyou vs. Van Brant, 2 Johns. N. Y., 357 ; Blundel vs. Caterall (English case) ; Ball vs. Slack, 2 Whart, Pen. It has been repeatedly ruled that where the language of description is bounded " by the *shore* of the bay," or " *shore* of the sound," as the case may be, the shore, that is the space between high and low water mark, is *excluded* from the grant ; and when the language is bounded " by the *Sound*," &c., the shore defined as above is *included* in the grant. Stover vs. Freeman, 6 Mass., R. 435 ; Cornfield vs. Coryell, 4 Wash. (Cir. Co.) R. 384. This important distinction was well understood by the crown lawyers who prepared charters and patents; " by the *shore* of the Sound " means one thing; " by the *Sound*," means another; yet the Court ignores this distinction and uses the terms indiscriminately, in the decision under consideration.

It is not disputed that in a private grant of land, using the terms bounded by the shore of specific waters, or wholly silent as to the water, the grant only runs to high water mark ; but it is a principle as old as the common law that waters within " known bounds" may be conveyed together with the dry land; that when they come within the body of the grant, as shown by appropriate words, they pass with the dry lands, especially when the grant, in addition to title, carries governing powers. We are at a loss to understand what more appropriate words the King could use for the purpose of granting havens, harbors, &c., than appears in the Patents to this Town. First—" the Sound" (not the shore of the Sound) is the northern boundary; next, the meadows, necks of land, &c., together with all harbors, havens, &c., within the before mentioned bounds; that is within the Sound. There was evidently an intent to pass all these waters. " When an intention appears to pass the thing, it shall pass." The fact that after the " Sound" was designated as the boundary, the instrument particularly enumerates the character of waters which shall be included in the grant, shows a purpose to leave no room for doubt or uncertainty as to the intent of the instruments; otherwise the use of these phrases " bays, havens, harbours," &c., are wholly meaningless.

The Patent from Governor Dongan was submitted to the Attorney-General for examination and received his approval, and the approval of the Council of the Colony, as appears upon its face. The Charters and patents were evidently drawn with care by law-officers, accustomed to prepare such documents, and it is fair to presume they used no more words, and no other terms, than were necessary and appropriate to effect the purpose designed.

The three Patents given the Town of Huntington are very similar in their terms to other grants made by Colonial Governors under authority of Kings of England, during the same period, to other towns, and to individual proprietors. We cannot discover that any of the grants to other towns have been construed by the Courts, upon the question of boundary, as the Huntington Patents were construed in the case above quoted of *Lowndes vs. Dickerson.* The grant under which the neighboring town of Oyster Bay successfully vindicated its right to the soil under tide waters, and an exclusive right of fishery therein, is no more favorable in its language to such right of soil and fishery than are the Huntington Patents to the latter Town. We refer to the case of *Rogers vs. Jones,* (1 Wendell, N. Y. 237.)

In 1677, Sir Edmond Andross, granted to Henry Townsend and six others, a territory bounded as follows: " Bounded on the north *by the Sound,* and on the east by the Huntington limits, on the south partly by the sea and partly by the Huntington limits; on the west by the boundaries of Hempstead, including all the necks of land and islands within the aforesaid prescribed bounds, with all marshes, waters, lakes, rivers, fishing, hunting, hawking, &c., with all the profits and emoluments to the tract belonging, and all the privileges and rights belonging to a township." By a regulation made by the people of Oyster Bay, at a town meeting, all persons, not residents of that Town were prohibited from taking oysters in any of the waters of that Town, under a penalty. The defendant, a non-resident of Oyster Bay Township, but a citizen of the State of New York, took and carried away one hundred oysters from a place in the Bay, one mile from Long Island Sound, about one hundred yards from the beach, and nearer Lloyd's Neck than any other land. Suit was brought on the part of the Town of Oyster Bay to enforce the penalty. Woodworth J. decided, " The Patent from Sir Edmond Andross, emanating mediately from Charles the Second, did convey to the inhabitants of Oyster Bay all the lands under water within the bounds of that grant, together with the exclusive right of fishing in the waters within the same." It will be noticed that the northern boundary is described by similar words with the Huntington Patent, viz. : " by the Sound." The particular description of waters to be included within the grant are less comprehensive than in the Huntington Patents; with " all marshes, lakes and rivers," it might with some reason be claimed, is not language appropriate to convey bays, harbors, creeks and coves; nevertheless the Court *held* that the Sound, proper, in the common meaning of the term, was the boundary; and that the arm of the sea, where the oysters were taken, was within the grant to the Town of Oyster Bay.

The case of *Sammis vs. Selleck*, brought up the question directly as to the rights of the Town of Huntington in tide waters. Selleck, under a lease from the Town, put down marine railways below high water mark in Huntington Harbor, below and adjoining lands of the plaintiff, Sammis. The latter brought an action of trespass ; but judgment was rendered for the defendant Selleck, and the rights of the Town, as claimed, were fully sustained. Judge Selah B. Strong, who rendered the decision in this case, held as follows : "I find that the Patent to the Town of Huntington conveyed to the Trustees of that Town, and their successors, in fee, the land covered with the navigable waters of Huntington Harbor." As to the adjacent owner, he says: "I find that the defendant's land was bounded by the shore of the harbor, and did not extend below ordinary high water mark." Though Judge Brown, in the case of *Lowndes vs. Dickerson*, affirms, in general terms, that the Town only owns to "the edge of the water," it is by no means clear that he would apply this construction to land-locked harbors like Huntington Harbor. The theory of that case seems to rest upon the supposition that there were nothing less than open arms of the sea on the north side of the Town, upon the shores of which the waters of the Sound washed, unobstructed by beaches, bars or headlands. Other principles of construction, not considered by the Court in that case, would apply to a grant of inland waters, like Huntington Harbor; and we cannot consider the case of *Sammis vs. Selleck* as overruled by *Lowndes vs. Dickerson*, but regard it as good authority as to the title of the Town in Huntington Harbor.

We think that under the charter of Charles the Second to the Duke of York, and the three subsequent grants to the Town of Huntington, title has been vested in the town to all the lands under tide water, on the north, as far out as the Sound opposite the headlands of Lloyd's and Eaton's Necks, thence eastward " by the Sound," on the line of ordinary low water mark, to the west boundary of Smithtown, including all the bays, harbors, coves, and creeks; and that the boundary on the south extends to low water mark on the ocean shore, including all lands under tide waters in the Great South Bay, its coves and creeks, and the mouths of its rivers. Any other construction placed upon the charters and grants will make a large part of these ancient documents a mass of worthless verbiage. Nevertheless, as long as the case of *Lowndes vs. Dickerson* stands without being overruled, it is the law, at least so far as the territory in issue in that case is concerned. It has judicially broken down the boundaries of the Town, boundaries that had for two hundred years been carefully guarded, as we have seen in our historical review, by repeated and long continued acts of exclusive use, ownership and jurisdiction. The case should have been carried to the Court of Appeals, but as it is too late for that, we think the Town should not rest contented under this decision, so destructive to its interests, and, as we conceive, so erroneous in its conclusions, but should seek the earliest opportunity of going before the Courts upon issues which will fairly test its rights to the ownership of the territory.

It must not, however, be assumed, provided the case of *Lowndes vs. Dickerson* is good law as to the particular locality involved in that case, that the Town owns no lands under tide waters. The case decides that Northport Harbor (more properly bay), is not in the Town of Huntington under the grant, but it does not necessarily follow that the inner harbors, coves, and creeks, may not be within the grant. These are inland waters almost entirely surrounded by land, and embrace such a limited territory at low tide, as to be little else than mud flats or shoals. The term " edge of the water," used by Judge Brown, must, upon every recognized principle of construction, mean the edge of the water at low tide. " By the Sound " includes the shore, at least, within the grant.

In conformity to the opinion heretofore expressed, that the King of England had power to grant, and did, through his subordinates, grant by virtue of the several charters and patents heretofore mentioned, to the Town of Huntington, title to the soil under all the tide waters within the line of ordinary low water mark on Long Island Sound, on the north, and the Atlantic Ocean on the south, it follows that the Town now holds that title, in all of its parts where it has not granted it away. The records of the Town show how far and in what manner it has made grants of land. Riparian owners hold only to the line of ordinary high water mark ; such was the common law of England when this country was settled, and such is now the law of this State. To extend their ownership down into and under the flow of tide water they must show a grant, or claim by prescription, which is presumptive of a grant.

In the case of *Commonwealth vs. Charlestown* (1. Pick. Mass. R. 180), the Court says: " The doctrine of common law is that the right of the soil of the proprietors of land on navigable rivers extends only to high water mark." Excepting where grants have been made by the Town to individual owners, the Town stands invested with title to the soil under tide waters within its boundaries, and its Trustees are invested with authority to control, manage and dispose of the same, subject to the public rights of navigation, to be hereafter considered.

So far, these investigations relate to an inquiry into the question as to how far out under tide water the Town owns the soil, and we have treated of this branch of the subject first, because, if the Town owns no lands under tide water by virtue of its grants, it can make no manner of difference how ownership in such lands are affected or qualified by the rights of the public in and over such soil and waters. If it owns no lands flowed by tide waters, the title must be in the State of New York, by virtue of its sovereignty, or in the grantees of the latter, and it would be idle to discuss the great public rights of navigation and fishing. Having, however, concluded that the Town does own lands under tide waters, by virtue of its grants from the Crown of England, we now proceed to discover, if possible, how, if at all, this ownership is qualified by the rights of the public, or the power of the State, in its sovereign capacity, in order to determine how far and in what manner the Trustees of the Town may control, manage, and dispose of this species of property.

While the King of England held the soil of all navigable rivers and arms of the sea, and the sea itself, to the distance of a cannon shot from the shores, he held it subject to the right of navigation, the right of all his subjects to pass over such waters in vessels and boats, in the pursuit of all legitimate purposes of commerce, the same as they might pass over all public highways on the dry land with wagons, carriages and all kinds of vehicles, title to such dry lands being at the same time in a private individual. Such was the law when the grants were made, and the Town received these town lands subject to this great right of public easement, and it can do nothing to obstruct or materially impair the right.

By the Common Law, as long as the soil under tide waters is held by the King or by the State, it is so held subject to the right of the people of the realm, or the state, as the case may be, to fish in the waters that flow over it. Lord Hale says: "The King is lord of the great waste of the sea, subject to certain beneficial rights of fishing and navigation, immemorially enjoyed by his subjects therein by the custom of the realm, which is the common law." The reason of the law seems to be discovered in the fact that the deep and remote sea is incapable of being utilized and reduced to individual possession; nevertheless, as is held by Bracton, those parts of the sea lying near the shore may be capable of individual improvement, occupation and profit: and as to such parts the reason of the rule ceases and the law ceases.

In an old English case, reported 1 Mod., 21 Charles, p. 106, the common law rule is plainly stated as follows:—"In case of a navigable river the lord having the soil, it is good evidence to prove that he hath the right of fishing, and it puts the proof upon them that claim *liberam piscareum*. But in case of a river that flows and reflows, and is an arm of the sea, then *prima facie* it is common to all, and if any will appropriate a privilege to himself the proof lieth on his side, f r in case of an action of trespass br ught for fishing there, it is *prima facie* a good justification to say that the *locus in quo* is *brachium marinus unusqui domi regis habet et habere debet liberum piscarium.* In the River Severn there are particular restraints, but the soil doth belong to the lords on either side, and a special sort of fishery belongs to them likewise, but the common sort of fishery is common to all. The soil of the river Thames is in the King, and the Lord Mayor is conservator of the river, and it is common to all fishermen, therefore there is no such contradiction betwixt the soil being in one and yet the river being common to all fisheries."

To the claim of any citizen of the State of New York to fish in the waters within the grants to the Town of Huntington, upon the ground of having a common right of fishery, the Town would have to interpose the plea of a special, exclusive fishery, and bring into Court the badges of such right, viz.: The charters and grants under which it claims. The three several Patents of the Town in express words convey to the Town "all fishing, hawking, hunting," &c., within the boundaries prescribed. That the intent was to convey to the Town an exclusive fishery, we think there can be no reasonable doubt. If it be contended that nothing more was intended to be conveyed than the right of a common fishery, the answer is that no words whatever were necessary to convey a common fishery. A common fishery in all the seas, and arms of the sea, where an exclusive one was not lawfully held, was the common birthright of every Englishman. It would therefore have been an idle mockery for the Sovereign, in the solemn form of a grant, to seek to convey to the people what they already held without a grant. If the words "all fishing," &c., are construed as conveying a common fishery, the grant is, in that respect, void.

"Although a several fishery in an arm of the sea may be prescribed for, and may pass as a privilege appurtenant to an estate, yet a prescription for a common fishery therein, as appurtenant to an estate, is bad. Thus in *Ward vs. Cresswell* (Willis' R., 265), the Court held, that as all the subjects of England might of common right, fish in the sea, &c., a prescription for it, as appurtenant to a particular township, was void, and as absurd as a prescription would be for traveling the King's highway as appurtenant to a particular estate." *Angell on Tide Waters, p.* 274.

" Where a grant of the King may be taken to two intents, one good and the other not, it should be construed to such intent as makes the grant good." *King vs. Bishop of Chester,* (4 *Mod., p.* 301).

A grant, or prescription, of a common fishery being bad, we should construe the words: "all fishing," &c., in the grant under consideration, as conveying an *exclusive* fishery, that being " such an intent as makes the grant good," under the rule above quoted.

This brings us to the question whether, although the King intended to convey an exclusive fishery, he really had power to do so. For, however ready he may have been to grant an exclusive fishery to the people of the Town of Huntington, and however clear and appropriate the terms employed in the instrument, for that purpose, if there were no power to do the thing sought to be done, the grants are, in that respect void, and no right of exclusive fishery is thereby vested in the Town.

The question whether the King, since *Magna Charta,* can grant an exclusive fishery, has greatly occupied the attention of lawyers and the courts for the last five hundred years. The authorities are conflicting. On the part of those who deny the right, it is claimed that, although formerly the King had the right, yet by the sixteenth section of *Magna Charta,* passed in the ninth year of Henry the Third, the King was debarred of that right, and that ever since no exclusive or several fisheries have been granted, other than by act of Parliament; or, if such have been granted, they are void. On the other hand, it is claimed, that *Magna Charta* only restrained the King from putting the public fisheries " in defence " for his own exclusive use and enjoyment, as had been heretofore done as to the royal fisheries of the River Banne, but did not restrain him from granting exclusive fisheries to his subjects, as he had hitherto been accustomed to do. The authorities cited to sustain this construction are: 2 *Black. Com.,* 39;

Cruise's Digest, 201, title Franchise; Duke of Somersett vs. Fogwell, 2 Burn. & Cress, 875; 1 Statutes Great Britain and Ireland, 570, 718; 2 ib., 213, 242, 641, 648; 7 Coke's Rep., part 13, p. 35, 36. It is also claimed that if the construction above stated, was ever placed on the sixteenth section of Magna Charta, it had in such sense, long before the grants under which Huntington claims were made, become obsolete, and that the King continued afterwards to make such grants without an act of Parliament, and that such grants were upheld. Another answer is, that Magna Charta is a mere statute, and its application was local and confined to the realm of England, for which the Parliament, which passed it, was the local legislature, unless subsequently expressly extended to the Colonies by competent authority.

Much reliance has been placed on the old English case of Warren vs. Mathews, (as Reported in 6 Mod. 73,) where it is said: "Every subject of common right may fish with lawful nets," &c., "in navigable rivers as well as in the sea, and the King's grant cannot bar them thereof." On the other hand it is claimed, on high authority, that this report of the case is a mistake; That the Court intended to speak only of the right of the case in hand—that the King's grant, in that case, did not, or could not, bar the subject, because it was a defective grant; or that for other reasons than a want of power in the King to grant an exclusive fishery, the grant under consideration did not bar the right of common fishery. This is said to be the only case to be found in which the broad proposition is stated that the King's grant cannot bar the subject of the common right of fishery. Afterwards the King's Bench, in the case of Carter vs. Murcott, (4 Burr. R. 2162,) did not recognize the doctrine of Warren vs. Mathews, above referred to, Justice Yates, in Davis's report, says: "It is agreeable to the law that the crown may grant a several fishery in navigable rivers, where the sea flows and reflows, and in an arm of the sea."

The King has made grants of several and exclusive fisheries since Magna Charta, and these grants have been sustained and may be sustained, in proof of which we refer to Darr. Rep. 155. Donegal vs. Hamilton, 3; 3 Ridgway's parliamentary cases, 270, 328; 5 Cruise's Digest, 45, sec. 16, tit. 54, King's grant; Carter vs. Murcott, 4 Burr., Rep. 2163; 1 Mod., Rep. 105; Com. Dig. 108, tit. Navigation; 4 Coke., Rep., pt. 7, p. 19; Ballrooke vs. Gooden, 2 Burr., 1768; The Bankers case, Skinner's Rep. 601; The Mayor of Oxford vs. Richardson, 4 Dunford and East., 436; 5 Burr. 285, 5 Mod. 556; 3 Barn and Cress, 875.

Among the American cases which sustain the right of the King to make such grants we cite the following: 2 Binney's Rep. 476; 4 Mass. Rep. 144, 522; 1 Pick. 180; 3 Johns. Rep. 367; 6 Johns. 131; 17 Johns. 195; 20 Johns. 90; 1 Conn. R. 284; 7 Conn. Rep. 480; 2

Conn. Rep. 481; 1 Hac. & Mellen. 504; 8 Wheat. 577, 597. Justice Thompson of the United States Supreme Court, in the case of *Martin vs. Waddell*, says: "The doctrine as laid down in the case of *Carter vs. Murcott* is universally recogniz d as the settled law on the subject and is fully adopted and sanctioned by the Courts of this country. Numerous cases of this description have come before the Courts of the State of New York and the principles and rules as laid down in the case of Carter vs. Murcott are fully recognized and adopted. In the case of *James and Gould*, 6 Cowen, 376, the Court in referring to that case place the decision upon it and say: "This is the acknowledged law of Great Britain and of this State and cases are referred to showing such to be the settled law."

Though the question is involved in some difficulty we believe that the weight of authority is on the side that the King may, since *Magna Charta*, grant an exclusive fishery in the realm of England. Yet if there were doubts as to the power of the King to make such grants, within the realm, we think that all reasonable room for doubt upon the subject disappears with respect to his power to grant an exclusive fishery in the old Colony of New York. Long Island, and its waters, never formed any part of the realm of England, upon which the pretended prohibition of *Magna Charta* could operate, unless its provisions were expressly extended and applied to the Colony. Charles the Second, by his Charter to the Duke of York, pursuant to the inherent power in the Sovereign to establish and maintain order, and the rights of property among his subjects in distant colonies, made a grant of political power under which the Colony could, and did organize a local law making a body of their own, competent to make laws for the government of the Colony, as Parliament made laws for the realm of England. If a ratifying act of Parliament was essential to give validity to a grant by the King of an exclusive fishery within the realm, the legislature of the Colony of New York could, pursuant to its powers, lend the like sanction and force to a grant within the territories of such Colony. The Colonists always claimed such power and authority over their own local concerns, denied such authority in Parliament, and the war of the Revolution was fought to vindicate this principle.

Under the powers of government, conferred through the charter, the people of the Colony could, in their discretion, change the common law of England upon the subject of the common right of fishery, in the same manner that they changed it upon other subjects. The people of the Town of Huntington always claimed the power, under their respective charters and grants, to an exclusive fishery within the limits of their grant. Long after they had claimed and exercised these rights, through orders made at town meetings, and otherwise, the Colonial Assembly of the Colony, in 1691, passed an Act entitled "An Act for settling, quieting, and confirming, unto the cities, towns, manors, and freeholders, within this Province, their several grants, patents, and rights, respectively." This act ratified and confirmed the patents or grants, heretofore made to the Town of Huntington. Section First declares: "That all the charters, patents, and grants, made, given, and granted, under the seal of this Province, constituted and authorized by their late and present Majesties, the Kings of England, and registered in the Secretaries Office, unto the several respective corporations, or bodies politick, of the cities, towns, and manors, and also to the several and respective freeholders within this Province, are, and forever shall be deemed, esteemed, and reputed, good and effectual charters, patents, and grants, authentic in the law," &c. Section Second declares: "That all the charters, patents, and grants, made, given, and granted, as aforesaid, unto all and every, the several and respective corporations, or bodies politick, of the cities, towns, and manors, and their successors, and also unto all and every, the respective freeholders, their heirs and assigns, forever within this Province, are, to all intents and purposes whatsoever, hereby ratified and confirmed, to have, hold, exercise, occupy, possess, and enjoy, all their, and every of their, *former rights, customs, privileges, preheminencies, practices, immunities, liberties, franchises, royalties, and usages, whatsoever*," &c. We submit that this act not only amounts to a ratification of the grants, and in that respect is equivalent to a ratifying Act of Parliament with respect to similar subjects within the realm, but it sanctioned all "of those" former rights, customs, and usages, which had heretofore obtained in the Colony, as well those which were not in accordance with the common law of England as such as did conform to it. The immemorial custom of the people of the Town of Huntington, in maintaining an exclusive fishery within its waters, is one of the customs thus sanctioned, no matter how repugnant it may have been to the common law, public right of fishery.

The principle that the Colonies might change the common law of England in respect to rights of this nature has never been denied. Under the common law riparian owners own to the line of high water mark only. In Massachusetts, a Colonial Legislature enacted, that, owners adjoining tide waters should own to low water mark. The common law was abrogated, and a new rule established, which has been maintained to this day. The same was the case in Connecticut, and other States. The Supreme Court of the United States, in the case of *Cornfield vs. Coryell*, 4 Wash. Cir. Co. R. 384, fully recognized this principle, and applied it to the case of the boundaries of New Jersey. The Court said: "The only objection which could have been opposed to the exercise of those acts of ownership under this grant, was that the Duke had himself no title to the Bay and River Delaware, under the royal grant to him. But the presumption is, nevertheless, irresistible, that the benefits intended to be bestowed by this grant, *and which were confirmed by the other Acts of the Provincial Government*, before noticed, were considered by the inhabitants of the Province as being too valuable not to be enjoyed by them. This use of the bay and river amounted to an appropriation of the water so used, and this title became, as has before been observed, indefeasable by the treaty of peace," &c.

When, therefore, the Town of Huntington brings into Court its several charters and patents from the Kings of England, sanctioned and confirmed by the Colonial Council, and the Colonial Assembly, its titles and rights are invested with the badges of all the appropriate political powers, executive and legislative, within or without the Colony, and the rights thus acquired became indefeasable by the treaty of peace with Great Britain and the constitution and laws of the State of New York.

It is said that ownership of soil and an exclusive fishery may be established by prescription, custom and usage which, if ancient enough, becomes law and supports title. The Courts of this and other States have upheld claims to an exclusive fishery founded on prescription. It was so in the case of James and Gould, under which the owners in Lloyd's Manor maintained an exclusive fishery in the waters of Lloyd's Harbor, adjoining their lands. But prescription is founded on the presumption of a grant; and if no grant of any exclusive fishery could be made by the King since *Magna Charta*, in the thirteenth century, how can one be presumed, in this country, which was not discovered until long after that time? It can hardly be said that we may presume a valid grant by act of parliament, and thus maintain title and exclusive fishery by prescription, for there are no facts or records upon which to found such a presumption within the limits of the old Colony of New York. No such grants were made. Therefore, an exclusive fishery in this country, founded on prescription, necessarily presumes that such exclusive grant came from the King, since *Magna Charta*, and that such grants are good. As a learned judge remarks: "we may as well, for all practical purposes, in this country, presume a grant since the beginning of the world as before *Magna Charta*."

Independently of this, there is good authority for maintaining that, inasmuch as by the several grants to the Town, title to the soil became vested in it, to all these lands under water, the grants passed everything susceptible of private and individual ownership of which, at least, shell-fishing is one. A distinction is made between shell-fish and floating fish. Perhaps the soil under tide waters may be in one and a common, or an exclusive fishery, as to floating fish be in others; but as to shell-fish the case is different. The soil is essential to their existence. They are a growth and product of the soil to an equal extent as vegetation on the dry land; they cannot be separated from the soil without destruction, any more than floating fish can be separated from the water without destruction. They are susceptible of a higher and more enduring character of ownership. Floating fish cease to be the exclusive property of their captors, in public waters, as soon as returned to their element, while property in shell-fish continues wherever they may be lawfully planted and cultivated. This susceptibility to be reduced to utility and continued ownership, nearness to the shores, and dependence upon the soil, makes shell-fish a part and parcel of the soil, not to be severed therefrom against the will of the owner of the soil.

Justice Thompson of the United States Supreme Court, very clearly states this distinction in his opinion in the case of *Martin vs. Waddell*. Though a dissenting opinion, his views upon this particular point do not appear to be in conflict with the opinion of the Court in that case. He says : " With respect however to the right of fishery, there is, in my judgment, a marked distinction, both in reason and authority, between the right in relation to floating fish and the right of dredging for oysters. The latter is entirely local and connected with the soil. There are natural beds of oysters; but in other places there is a peculiar soil adapted to the growing of oysters. They are planted and cultivated by the hand of man like other productions of the earth ; and the books in many cases clearly hold up a distinction and speak of the oyster fishing as distinct from that of floating fish, 5 Burr. 2814 ; and in the case of Rogers and others v. Allen, Camp. Rep. 309, this distinction is expressly taken. It was an action of trespass for breaking and entering the several oyster fishery of the plaintiff in Burnham River, and fishing and dredging for oysters. The defence set up was that the *locus in quo* was a navigable river in which all the King's subjects had a right to fish and dredge for oysters, and evidence was introduced showing that all who chose had been accustomed to fish in Burnham River for all sorts of floating fish, without interruption ; and it was contended that a fishery was entire, and that as it had been proved that it was lawful for all the King's subjects to catch floating fish, so they might lawfully dredge for oysters. But Heath, Justice, ruled otherwise and said : a fishery was divisible, a part may be abandoned and another part of more value may be preserved. The public may be entitled to catch floating fish in the River Burnham, but it by no means follows that they are justified in dredging for oysters, which may still remain private property ; and although a new trial was granted upon another point in the case, the doctrine as above stated was not at all impugned by the Court of King's Bench."

The public right to dig for shellfish in a part of the shore, which had become private property, was recognized in the case of *Bogart vs. Orr*, 3 *Boss. & Pull R.*, 472, in England, but Kent considers this case overruled in the celebrated case of *Blundell vs. Catterall*, before referred to. The law of this State, as construed in the case of *James vs. Gould* (the Lloyd's Manor case), is certainly against the existence of such a public right. Angell concludes that ownership of the soil supports a claim to a private or several fishery, but that is is essential that the owner, and the former owner, of such soil should have immemorially excluded the public by means of a several fishery, prescribed and proved, or guaranteed in express ancient grant.

Whatever may have been, or may be the power of the King, as to granting an exclusive or several fishery in the tide waters within the realm of England, we think we may safely conclude, that by virtue of the charter from Charles the Second to the Duke of York, in 1663, and the three several patents or grants to the Town, dated respectively 1666, 1688 and 1694, ratified by Act of the Colonial Legislature, and strengthened by immemorial custom, a valid title is vested in the Town of Huntington to the lands covered by the tide waters of its bays, harbors, creeks and coves, and the shores thereof, and that it has an exclusive fishery in all such waters.

The Act of the Legislature, passed in 1823, empowers the Town, in its corporate capacity, to make and enforce rules and regulations concerning the management, improvement, and disposal of its lands and property. We think it competent for the Trustees, in behalf of the Town, under such regulations as it may make, to lease those lands under water for the cultivation of oysters, in the usual way, upon such terms, and in such manner, as will best conserve the interests of the residents of the Town; and that the Town can protect its grantees in the exclusive and quiet enjoyment of such property. That it can exclude non-residents of the Town, who have not acquired vested rights in such waters, from participation in these privileges. That it may hold, for the exclusive use of its own inhabitants, all fisheries within its limits, whether of shell fish or floating fish, and may protect and preserve these fisheries by prohibiting the use of unlawful nets, weirs, dredges, or other destructive instruments, whether in the hands of non-residents or residents of the Town.

It must not be presumed that the Town, however valid its title to the lands under water, and to an exclusive fishery therein, has unlimited control of the subject. The State, by virtue of its sovereignty may, through the Legislature, prescribe rules as to the manner of enjoying the use of the fisheries; it may prohibit fishing at certain times of the year favorable to incubation, and may regulate the character and mode of using any and all kinds of decoys, or instruments used in seizing and appropriating this class of property. Its game laws invade private property on dry land, and prescribe the manner of the use of all animals which come within the purview of such laws ; and its authority over shell fish and floating fish in this respect is equally supreme, whether the Town owns the lands under water or not ; the power of the Town over the same subject is concurrent with that of the Legislature to a cert..in extent, but also subordinate to it. In the absence of State laws it may make regulations, or it may at all times, under the act of 1823, make rules concerning the subject, not in conflict with the laws of the State. In the foregoing observations we refer to the *manner of the use and enjoyment* of these fisheries, *not the right to the property ;* that is indefeasible, and cannot be taken from the Town by any power in the State without the consent of people of the Town.

A brief abstract of laws, passed by the State upon the subject of the fisheries, may not be inappropriate.

The State has, at different times, provided by statute that the inhabitants of certain towns may enjoy an exclusive oyster fishery in the public waters of the same, requiring persons who avail themselves of its privileges, to clearly mark out and designate by stakes, the quantity of land taken, usually restricted from three to five acres to each person ; prohibiting the occupation of grounds having a natural growth of oysters, and requiring a rent to be paid to the Town for such use. See Session Laws, 1864, p. 1320; 1808, p. 1052 ; 1803, p. 838.

Some of these laws are now in force, and some have been superseded by others. In 1870, an Act was passed with the following title : "An Act for the preservation of shell-fish in the waters of South Bay, in Suffolk County." 1st. It prohibits any person from dredging for any purpose, at any time. 2d. Prohibits taking oysters, or any kind of shell-fish, between sun set and sun rise, and between the 15th day of June and the 15th day of September, in each year, with severe penalties for violation of its provisions.

The State unquestionably has the right to regulate the manner of the use of fisheries, whether in tide waters, or the inland rivers, and to prohibit the use of destructive instruments calculated to diminish the annual increase, or their taking during certain periods of the year, and has exercised this right. See 1 Ed. R. S., p. 040. The passage of this Act is, therefore, not inconsistent with the ownership and authority of this Town over the same territory.

So an Act was passed in 1865, forbidding the use of purse nets, and some other kind of nets, near portions of the South Beach in this Town. In some cases the State has given the owners of adjoining lands the exclusive privilege of staking off oyster beds, and using such soil without any compensation; this has been confined to the public waters of the State, and not permitted within the limits of any existing grant. See 4 Ed. R. S., p. 94.

An Act passed in 1871, prohibits the use of purse nets, in any of the waters within the jurisdiction of this State, lying easterly of the boundary between Queens and Suffolk Counties, except the waters of Long Island Sound, Gardner's Bay, and Little Peconic Bay, under a penalty of two hundred dollars for each offense. In the case of Lowndes v. Dickerson, we have seen that Judge Brown held that "Long Island Sound" properly embraced all the tide waters on the Sound running inland as far as the tide ebbs and flows. If the same construction is applied to the above statute, concerning the use of purse nets, there would be no waters within the territory described in the Act on the north side of this Town upon which the law could operate. The absurdity of such a construction is manifest.

In 1840 an Act was passed giving Boards of Supervisors power to make laws for the preservation of game and shell-fish, and other fish, and all acts then existing upon the subject were repealed. Since that time the State has enacted the laws above referred to, the most of which are embodied in the Act of 1871.

The conclusions arrived at by us upon the subject of the title of the Town in lands under tide waters, and the right of fishery in such waters, are not in accordance with the opinion of the Court in the case of *Lowndes vs. Dickinson,* and inasmuch as this case arose out of and directly affects these waters, and has the force of a judicial determination, we are of the opinion that the Town is not at present in a position to enter upon an extended system of leasing oyster grounds. Grave questions may arise as to vested rights acquired in consequence of this unfortunate decision, and while the Town should firmly assert its rights, and protest against the invasion of its property under the authority of this decision, and seek the earliest opportunity of having their rights again adjudicated by the Courts, it should proceed cautiously, and in a way to avoid a great number of lengthy and vexatious suits, which would be likely to result from any general system of leasing oyster lands at this time. Let one case be made which will fairly test the rights of the Town, and if necessary carry it through to the Court of Appeals; then, if the decision should be adverse, the Town will have to abide the result; on the other hand if favorable to the Town, as we think it would be, it would then be in a position to lease the lands in such way as to protect the rights of those in occupation, so far as they were entitled to protection, and secure to the Town a large revenue which is at present wholly lost; or the Town may invoke the aid of the Legislature of the State, and seek to forever set all these questions at rest, by an Act granting to the Town of Huntington all the right, title and interest of the State of New York, in and to the lands under the tide waters, now claimed to be within the boundaries of the Town; designating such territory by courses and distances, or in other appropriate ways, so that no dispute could arise as to the true limits, and granting to the Town an exclusive fishery therein. We should deem any legislation which came short of this, as inadequate to the purposes required. As we are of the opinion that the Town already holds this title, of right, and can successfully vindicate its rights in the Courts, we do not advise legislation, and only suggest it, as possible, in case the Town declines to avail itself of the former remedy.

### WHARFS AND DOCK LEASES.

The property in the shores and lands under tide-waters being in the Town, it has exclusive control as to the projection of wharves and docks into such tide-waters. By the common law, riparian owners have no right to project docks or piers from their lands into adjoining tide-waters, whether such structures impede navigation or not. When the King held title he could abate the intrusion. Lord Hale, says: "Where the soil is the King's, the building below high water-mark is a *purpresture,* an incroachment, an intrusion upon the King's soil, which he may demolish, or seize, or arrent, at his pleasure." Under the Charters and grants to the Town of Huntington, heretofore mentioned, it possesses the power over this subject, which formerly belonged to the King and would otherwise have been lodged in the State of New-York, and may abate such structures. The Town has the right to erect, or grant to others the right to erect, wharves and docks, and other structures, where they do not impede navigation, and the Town, or its grantees, may exact compensation from all persons who enter upon and use such property. As to the shore, which is the space between high and low water-mark, including the mud-flats and sedge-bottoms left bare by the ebb of tide, the Town may lay it off in lots, or such parcels as it chooses, and convey the same in fee simple, and its grantees may, by earth-fillings and sea-walls, convert the same into dry lands, for cultivation, or erect thereon any sort of lawful structure, saving only that navigation shall not thereby be impeded.

"When the State makes a grant of land covered with the waters of a bay, or navigable river, and the grantee reclaims and raises it above the surface of the water, it is not a mere franchise to collect wharfage, and belonging to the public at large for commercial purposes, but the grantee is invested with all the rights that pertain to the ownership of land. People vs. Kelcey. 38 Barb. 269. Here the Town standing in the place of the State, as to ownership and authority over tide-lands, its grants confer equal privileges.

But the Town cannot license the erection of docks and wharves opposite the lands of riparian owners, and secure to the public free access over such adjoining lands, against the consent of such riparian owner. The public have no right, either at common law, or by Statute, in this State, to pass over any part of the lands of a riparian owner, in going to or from a wharf, or other structure, projecting into navigable waters, without the consent of such riparian owner. In the case of Ledyard vs. Ten Eyck, 36 Barb. 126 ; the Court after stating that "under the civil law the banks of the public rivers and the sea shore were held to be public," affirms : " But such was not the common law in England, nor in this State. The public here have no highway along the margins of our navigable rivers and lakes, unless the same has been acquired by express grant or prescription."

In lands under tide-water belonging to the Town, "the State is trustee for the public so as to protect navigation, and prevent hinderences, and obstructions thereto" ; but its trusteeship for riparian owners, in that, grants of tide-waters adjacent to their premises shall be made to them, and none others, does not apply to these waters. It is a trusteeship declared by Statute, and only applicable to State lands. The privileges of riparian owners have however been carefully guarded, and conveyances and leases of tide lands, whether for wharf purposes, or for the use and enjoyment of the salt-grasses, or otherwise, have usually been made to adjacent owners, only.

The right of mooring vessels and of landing goods upon the lands of riparian owners, does not exist in this State, neither is it acquired by prescription, or long continued custom, with the knowledge of the owner. The true riparian owner may at any time assert his rights and exclude such use.

Since the case of Sammis vs. Selleck, we do not know that the right of the Town to exact compensation for the use of lands under water, in its harbors, has been seriously questioned, other than as the principles enunciated in Lowndes vs. Dickerson may affect such right. It leases lands for docks to the owners of adjoining lands, or opposite landing places, where the public have an easement, not otherwise, and in this respect it conforms to the course and practice adopted by the State. The commissioners of the Land Office are by Statute particularly restrained from making grants to any other than the proprietor of the adjacent land, and all of their grants are made upon two grounds : First, to promote commerce ; Second, that the land is proper for the beneficial enjoyment of the same by the owner. Though, in terms, the

Amendatory Act of 1835, extends the provisions of the Statute to the waters surrounding Long Island; the Act can of course only affect such lands under tide-waters as had not hitherto been granted, and cannot apply to such lands of this Town; nor is it any authority against the claims or title of the Town of Huntington. It applies to *all public waters*, within the boundaries designated, and never was intended to supersede the rights of owners, claiming under a valid grant. Riparian owners own to high water-mark, and no further, unless they can show a valid grant for the soil below that line. The Town owns all the shores and tide-waters below such line, which can reasonably come within the purposes of any wharf or other structure, and the State here has nothing to grant.

There are but two cases in this Town in which individuals have applied to and obtained grants from the Commissioners of the Land Office for wharves or docks; one is at Cold Spring, the other at Babylon. We believe these grants to be void. The Town of Huntington holds the exclusive right of making such grants, within its waters. With the growth of population and commerce, wharf and docking privileges are becoming more valuable, and the Trustees are required to use all reasonable diligence in preserving and protecting all the rights of the Town in its shores and waters.

The Town, where it has not parted with title, owns, and may by lease or sale, dispose of all stone, gravel, sand, beds of clay, minerals, (gold and silver mines excepted), grasses, or other valuable substances, incident to the soil, everywhere within its boundaries, below the line of high water mark, and all beaches and sand banks above high water mark, where they have not already been alienated; provided, it does not thereby impair navigation or injure the lands of riparian owners; and it is the duty of the Trustees to protect, preserve, and utilize all these various properties.

It may be safely assumed that the Trustees are the proper guardians and custodians of all the property belonging to the Town, other than where expressly excepted by law. That in behalf of, and for the Town, they have power to take, hold, manage, control, and convey real estate either for a term of years, or in fee simple; and to exercise the same rights as to all personal property, which, as Trustees, they may lawfully acquire and dispose of; and that all conveyances, or other writings, within the scope of their authority, as herein stated, properly executed by the President of the Trustees, duly authorized by the Trustees, and under the seal of the Town, are valid and binding upon all persons.